Woodrow, the White House Mouse

Written and illustrated by
Peter W. Barnes and
Cheryl Shaw Barnes

SCHOLASTIC INC.
New York Toronto London Auckland Sydney
Mexico City New Delhi Hong Kong

No part of this publication may be reproduced in whole or in part, or stored in a retrieval system, or transmitted in any form or by any means, electronic, mechanical, photocopying, recording, or otherwise, without written permission of the publisher. For information regarding permission, write to VSP Books, PO Box 17011, Alexandria, VA 22302.

ISBN 0-439-12952-4

Published by Scholastic Inc., 555 Broadway, New York, NY 10012, by arrangement with VSP Books.
SCHOLASTIC and associated logos are trademarks and/or registered trademarks of Scholastic Inc.

12 11 10 9 8 7 6 5 4 3 2 1   0 1 2 3 4 5/0

Printed in the U.S.A.   14

First Scholastic Trade paperback printing, February 2000

This book is dedicated to all the presidents,
First Ladies, and their families,
and men and women who have served
in the White House and executive branch—
thank you for your hard work and public service.
It is also dedicated to one of those women
in particular, Nancy Fleetwood Miller:
A special thank you for being a great
"campaign manager"—without you,
Woodrow would never have made it to the Oval Office!
—P.W.B. and C.S.B.

Acknowledgments
We want to thank Larry Householder,
for all his invaluable help and guidance;
Jim Miller, for letting Nancy out to play
all those early mornings and late nights;
Jim and Carole Kuhn, for the use of their great pictures;
two special friends, Kay Ryan and Susan Boardman,
for their continuous encouragement;
Jill Parker, and Meg and Stephen Upton,
for being great Easter egg rollers;
our families, for their love and support;
and our two wonderful daughters,
Maggie and Kate, for their patience—
we're back to normal now! (Almost...)
—P.W.B. and C.S.B.

Every four years, like the rest of us do,
    The mice of the nation elect someone, too.
Living in Washington's grandest old house,
    A leader respected--a President mouse!

Woodrow G. Washingtail won the last vote.
    "A mouse Yankee Doodle!" the newspapers wrote.
So good and so brave, and smart, if you please—
    His favorite food? Why, American cheese!

ELECT WOODROW FOR PRESIDENT

So on a cold winter's day, with most solemn respect,
Two presidents swore to preserve and protect
Our nation, our freedoms, our flag, see it wave—
Our land of the free and our home of the brave.

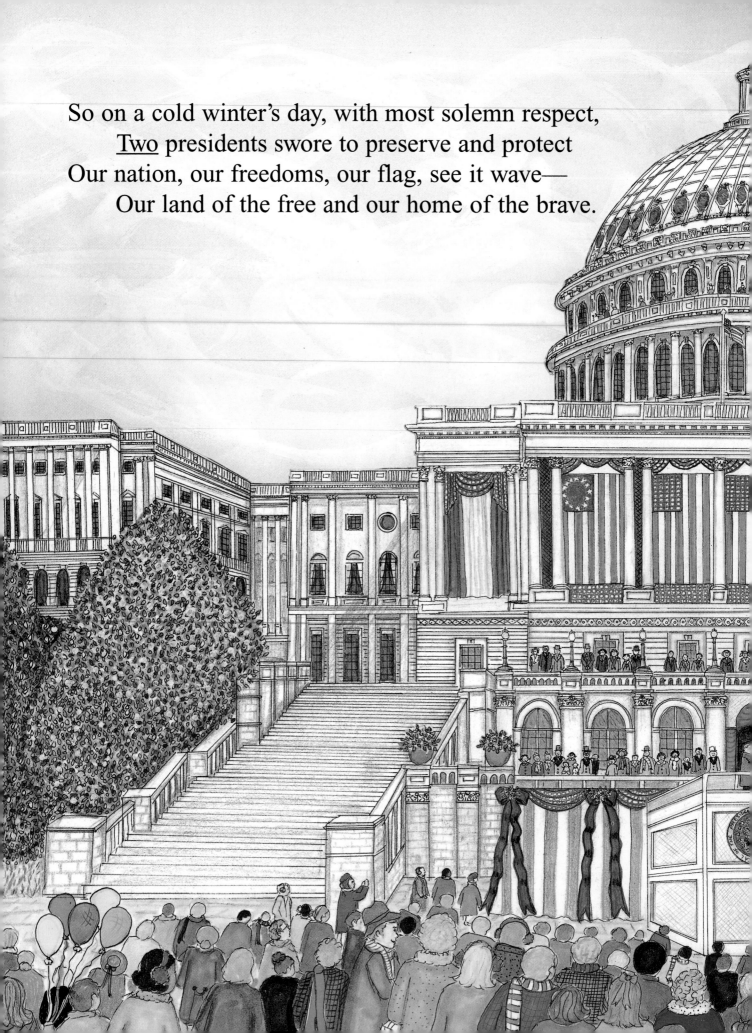

The White House was lit, floor to roof, wall to wall,
For the beautiful, splendid Inaugural Ball.

Soon, Woodrow arrived, with his First Lady, Bess,
And their children in tow—about eight, more or less.

There were Truman and Franklin, their two oldest sons,
And Quentin and Kermit, the mischievous ones.

And Dolley and Millie, and the twins, George and Art
(Not even their classmates could tell them apart).

The State Room was filled with good will and good cheer—
  The mouse children watched from the great chandelier.
It was going quite well, until George, with a whoop,
  Slipped and landed—ker-splash—in a senator's soup!

The President has a big job, you'll agree—
    Many places to go, many people to see.

In the great Oval Office, he does all his thinkin'—
And Woodrow, they say, is as smart as Abe Lincoln!

The President mouse has a desk on the shelf
  Where he works with his helpers or just by himself.
Our grand Constitution keeps a president busy—
  So many assignments, a mouse could get dizzy!

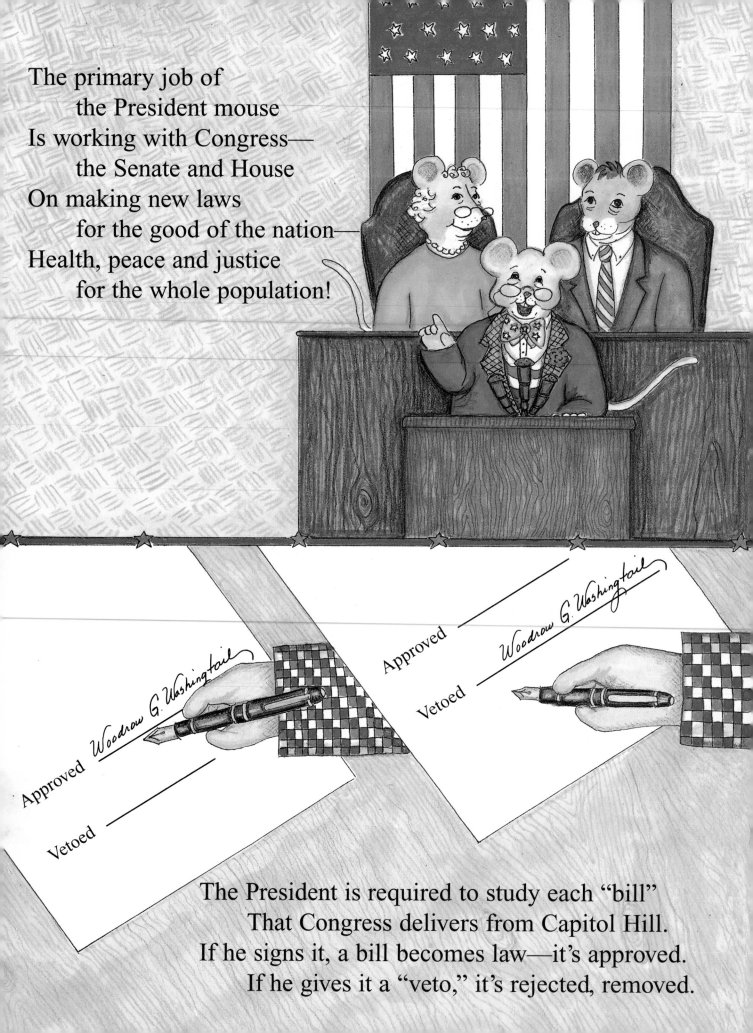

The primary job of
   the President mouse
Is working with Congress—
   the Senate and House
On making new laws
   for the good of the nation—
Health, peace and justice
   for the whole population!

The President is required to study each "bill"
   That Congress delivers from Capitol Hill.
      If he signs it, a bill becomes law—it's approved.
         If he gives it a "veto," it's rejected, removed.

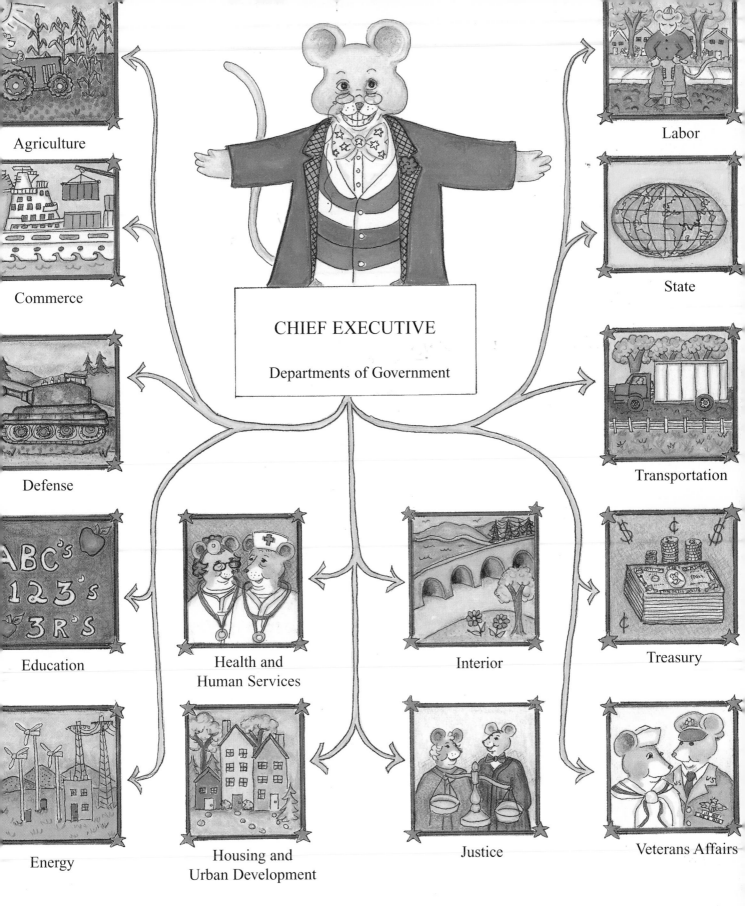

Agriculture

Commerce

Defense

Education

Energy

Labor

State

Transportation

CHIEF EXECUTIVE

Departments of Government

Health and
Human Services

Interior

Treasury

Housing and
Urban Development

Justice

Veterans Affairs

He's the "Chief Executive," which means he's in charge
Of government departments, the small and the large.
Government departments include Transportation,
Justice and Labor, and of course, Education.

He is also "Commander in Chief," and that means
The Army and Navy, Air Force and Marines
Report to the President as boss, the "Big Cheese"—
On this, every soldier and sailor agrees!

The President regularly talks with and greets
   The leaders from foreign countries he meets.
In this job, the President is our "Head of State"
   When handling foreign affairs, small and great.

But the President also gets time out to play—
Every Easter, for instance, is egg rolling day!
There are orange eggs, yellow eggs—purple eggs, too!
There are even some eggs colored red, white and blue!

Inside the White House,
  there's also more fun
For Woodrow, his family
  and most everyone!
The East Room is used
  for artistic events
Like concerts and shows
  for mouse ladies and gents!

One night, Millie dreamed that on one special day
    She might, if she practiced, dance an East Room ballet.
She'd be joined by the famous Marine Mouse Quartet
    For her flawless finale, a fine pirouette.

The Red Room and Green Room are not side by side,
But they're wonderful places for children to hide,
When they play hide and seek, and Woodrow is seeking—
But he finds them so fast—could it be that he's peeking?

The Blue Room at Christmas is decked to the ceiling
The fire is roaring—the children, all squealing,

Excited that Christmas is once again here,
To share with our loved ones and those we hold dear.

And as he nodded to sleep,
    the good President mouse
Was thankful for family
    and country (and house!).
"It's all so wonderful,"
    was his happy reflection,
"That a fellow just might
    want to seek re-election!"

Historical Notes for Parents and Teachers

The Presidency: After the United States became independent from England in 1783, the Founding Fathers did not want another king, with unchecked power, to run the young country. So in the Constitution, they divided power among three equal branches of government: The legislative (Congress), the judicial (Supreme Court) and the executive (President). The idea was to create a system of checks and balances, with no one branch dominating the other. To make changes and get things done, there had to be general agreement among all three.

The Constitution says that to be president, a person has to be at least 35 years old and a natural born American citizen. The president is elected every four years. He is allowed to serve only two four-year terms. The Constitution gives the president specific powers. As Chief Executive, he runs the government, enforcing laws and directing the many departments and agencies that implement them. He also is required to work with Congress on creating laws; not only does he make his own proposals for legislation, he must approve or reject (veto) proposed laws after they have passed Congress. Each year, the president goes to Congress to give the State of the Union address, a "report card" on the nation, to let everyone know how the country is doing. He also usually uses the address to propose his goals for the nation in the year ahead.

The president not only works with Congress, he also works with leaders of other countries, negotiating treaties and agreements, on trade, keeping peace and other issues of mutual interest. In this capacity, the president acts as our Head of State. As Head of State, he also is expected to be America's biggest cheerleader, upholding its traditions, dedicating monuments, presenting awards and participating in other ceremonial functions at home and abroad. Finally, the Constitution says the president is also the Commander in Chief of the nation's military, the Army, Navy, Air Force, Marines and Coast Guard.

Fun facts about presidents: The smallest was the fourth, James Madison, who was five feet, four inches tall and weighed less than 100 lbs. The tallest was the 16th, Abraham Lincoln, who stood six feet, four inches tall. The heaviest was the 27th, William Howard Taft, who was six feet, two inches tall and weighed more than 300 lbs. The president with the most children was the 10th, John Tyler, with 15. The oldest elected to the office was the 40th, Ronald Reagan, who was 69 when he took office. The youngest elected was the 35th, John F. Kennedy, who was 43. (Teddy Roosevelt, the 26th, was the youngest unelected president; as vice president, he succeeded to the office at the age of 41 upon the death of William McKinley in 1901.) The president who served the shortest term was the 9th, William Henry Harrison, who died of pneumonia a month after his inauguration. The longest-serving president was the 32nd, Franklin Roosevelt, who served just over 12 years.

The White House: When the Founding Fathers prepared their plans for a new federal city on the Potomac River, they included an Executive Mansion for the president. George Washington chose the site on which the mansion was built. In 1792, an Irish-born architect, James Hoban, won a competition to design it. In 1800, while it was still under construction, President John Adams moved in--presumably along with the first White House mice.

The mansion underwent many changes through the years. It had to be rebuilt after the War of 1812 (the British burned it). The south portico was added in 1824, and the north portico, in 1830. The West Wing was added in the early 1900s; the East Wing was constructed during World War II and included the first White House movie theater. A third floor was added to the main structure in 1927. During the Truman Administration, the house went through a major renovation.

Over the years, the building was called the President's House and the Executive Mansion. In 1901, Teddy Roosevelt officially changed the name to The White House.

Of the building's more than 100 rooms, several of the most famous are featured in this book. The State Room is used for the president's official dinners. The East Room--the largest room-- is used for entertaining, concerts, dances, press conferences and more. The Red Room serves as a parlor, as does the Green Room. The Blue Room is the main reception room. The Oval Office is where the president conducts official business.

In many of the book's illustrations, Cheryl Barnes has recreated the actual furnishings and decorations of those rooms. In the Oval Office illustration, for example, the president is seated at the "Resolute Desk," which was made from the oak timbers of the British ship *Resolute*. The desk was given as a gift to President Hayes by Queen Victoria in 1880, after the stranded ship was rescued by American whalers in the Arctic and returned to England.

Woodrow's First Lady and children have familiar names. Bess is named for Bess Truman. Woodrow's oldest son, Truman, is named for President Truman. Franklin is named for President Franklin Roosevelt. Quentin and Kermit were the names of two of the sons of Teddy Roosevelt. Dolley is named for Dolley Madison, First Lady to James Madison. Millie is the name of a springer spaniel owned by President George Bush. But George is named for George Washington, and Art, for Chester A. Arthur.

Anyone who has visited the Smithsonian Institution may recognize one of Bess's dresses in the book. At the Inaugural Ball, she is wearing the gown worn by Mamie Eisenhower, for the first inaugural for her husband, President Dwight D. Eisenhower, in 1953. It has 4,000 rhinestones and its pale pink color was soon known as "Mamie Pink." The dress is in the Smithsonian's collection of First Lady's gowns.

The annual Easter Egg Roll noted in the book was originally held at the Capitol. It moved to the White House in 1878, when President Hayes and his wife, Lucy, opened the South Lawn for the event. It is always held on the Monday after Easter.

For more information on the White House, contact or visit the White House Historical Association in Washington, D.C.

Three Bees

The Sound of EE

By Jody Jensen Shaffer

2

See the bees.

One. Two. Three.

5

6

Three bees fly free.

They fly on
the breeze.

8

The bees need sweet flowers.

The flowers are by trees and weeds.

14

Three bees find flowers.

The bees sip.

18

The bees fly home.

One. Two. Three.

20

21

Word List:

bees	sweet
breeze	three
free	trees
need	weeds
see	

Note to Caregivers and Educators

The books in this series are based on current research, which supports the idea that our brains are pattern-detectors rather than rules-appliers. This means children learn to read easier when they are taught the familiar spelling patterns found in English. As children encounter more complex words, they have greater success in figuring out these words by using the spelling patterns.

Throughout the series, the texts allow the reader to practice and apply knowledge of the sounds in natural language. The books introduce sounds using familiar onsets and *rimes*, or spelling patterns, for reinforcement.

For example, the word *cat* might be used to present the short "a" sound, with the letter *c* being the onset and "_at" being the rime. This approach provides practice and reinforcement of the short "a" sound, as there are many familiar words made with the "_at" rime.

The stories and accompanying photographs in this series are based on time-honored concepts in children's literature: well-written, engaging texts and colorful, high-quality photographs combine to produce books that children want to read again and again.

Dr. Peg Ballard
Minnesota State University, Mankato

The Child's World®
childsworld.com

Published by The Child's World®
1980 Lookout Drive • Mankato, MN 56003-1705
800-599-READ • www.childsworld.com

PHOTO CREDITS
© AlinaMD/Shutterstock.com: 13; Darios/Shutterstock.com: 2; giedre vaitekune/Shutterstock.com: 18; Inmt24/Shutterstock.com: 10; irin-k/Shutterstock.com: cover, 6; Petr Smagin/Shutterstock.com: 21; Protasov AN/Shutterstock.com: 14, 17; symbiot/Shutterstock.com: 9; weter78/Shutterstock.com: 5

ISBN 9781503835399
LCCN 2019944830

Printed in the United States of America

ABOUT THE AUTHOR

Jody Jensen Shaffer has written dozens of books for children. She also publishes poetry, stories, and articles in children's magazines. When she's not writing, Jody copy edits for children's publishers. She lives in Missouri.